PSYCHIC GAMBLES

by Aleks Stajkovic Jr.

aleksstajkovicjr.com

Strange Moon Press LLC
10 Benning Street
Suite 160-168
West Lebanon, NH 03784
www.strangemoonpress.com

I made four parlays in a row; the first one on Saturday and the last on Tuesday. None of them won. When you start down that path, it's hard to stop. But eventually, you gotta look your banking app square in the face and call it quits— or come up with a contingency plan— before you lose every-thing. The parlays were for baseball, MLB— the playoffs.

I didn't grow up in a household that played or watched baseball. I never particu-larly cared to watch sports for that matter, but I enjoyed baseball with money on the line, or against the spread, or on the over, but never the under. I had fooled myself with the notion that baseball was the best sport to bet on based off of a lucky baseball-heavy parlay a few months back. My strat-egy was to limit each parlay to three or four games and bet on the favorite for each of those combinations. Every time the favorite lost, my blood would boil.

Gambling never *seemed* to follow probability, at least not in my favor. A loss was often followed by a lengthy session of what my overweight ginger friend from childhood referred to as 'me time,' and this time was no different. In that protracted moment of bliss I forgot my several losses, none of which I could afford. Then came the sting of defeat ensued with full force, reminding me of my poverty, not befitting of my upbringing, and the money spent on me.

I've been told only a poor man gambles, but frankly, I didn't care if I were poor, nor if gambling suggested I was. I had bigger aspirations and was inching toward them; my net worth was of no concern. But still, I needed to satiate my material thirst in the interim to amend for an unwisely accrued debt since moving to the City of Angels.

Sports gambling had become my attempted solution, as well as my main source of income.

I zipped up, threw on some shoes and stepped outside. I lived in a guest room in a

residential home, which was sort of de-
tached from the main house. The path from
my room to the front gate was consistently
littered with old garden supplies, lawn
gnomes, and unused cleaning accessories.
The windows of the main house were always dark, but sometimes, if I stared long
enough, I could make out piles of various
items boxed together in neat rows.

I could never look for long because of
the smell; smatterings of canine fecal matter
could be found with each step on the pave-
ment, accompanied by tiny clusters of flies
buzzing above.

When I first visited the place I saw
about a dozen Shi-Tzus on the front lawn,
barking in a perfect cacophony. I asked the
owner, a single woman in her forties who
worked as a nurse, if she bred the dogs. She
looked at me like I was some sort of idiot.

Though my dwelling was small and
compact and was surrounded by several
small, aggressive dogs and owned by a se-
rial hoarder, I liked it. I had my own room
and outhouse for a relatively cheap rent,

which allowed me to afford it almost entirely off of my sports gambling.

Location-wise, it was something of an upgrade from my past homes out here. Not seeing a homeless person immediately upon exiting my domicile was a new experience to me, one that my then-current lodging offered, a stark contrast to the several dwellings in LA that I had inhabited prior.

It was a muggy August afternoon. Just around the corner was a string of cafes in a neighborhood called Silverlake, which was known to be 'hipster,' which actually meant it was predominantly inhabited by whites who wore baggy, expensive clothing and paid a premium for coffee.

I spent the rest of the day walking, passing by my eccentric, bohemian neighbors—a sort of therapeutic ritual to briefly escape from the clutches of compulsive gambling. It felt good to walk broke, empty-handed. I think it gave me a sense of vitality in going about my day. The way people looked at me, the thrill with each step—it all affected me positively.

At night, I went to a bar in Hollywood to drink with my friend Kester, who had been my college roommate. He was the first among my friends to put on the hefty mass I assumed would befall all of us eventually.

Whereas my goal to find work as an actor brought me to California, the state's large defense market lured Kester, an engineer by training. We settled at a dimly lit dive bar on Sunset Boulevard, which, as most did in the area, contrived for a sort of seventies aesthetic. There was a defunct cigarette machine bolted into the wall at the entrance, and on a counter by the restrooms, I saw a couple of milk crates full of vinyl records in tattered sleeves. All the while, music from obscure bands of the era like Mountain and Foghat played from the sound system. None of it felt real, but I still liked it.

By the time I started my second IPA, Kester was polishing off his third. He held up the bottle to his face, studying it, then looked at me. "What would happen if you brought a Heineken Zero to work?" he asked. "Crack open a cold one at your desk and start sipping away? I think they'd still get on your case. Even though technically there's no alcohol in it, maybe like half a percent, if anything."

I shrugged. I probably agreed, but chose not to engage the subject, which seemed to upset him.

"Look who I'm asking," he said with a short, tense laugh, before downing the rest of his drink. He would likely imbibe another seven or so back home, not that he couldn't afford them at the bar, unlike me. Compared to him, I might have as well been a teetotaler; I'd go days without drinking. Kester's nightly intake of alcohol was the same, regardless of the venue, and yet somehow, he never had a problem showing up to work the next morning.

I grabbed my bottle in one hand and with the other swiveled it around the surface of my palm. It was light, about an eighth of the beer left; the cool condensation from my inaugural sips had turned into a warm unsettling dampness that found its way into my grasp. Time for another, I thought. At some point in my tenure as a beer drinker, I stopped finishing my beers; instead of taking the last few swigs I would move on to a new one.

Kester started to explain that his office was renovating their building, which apparently was going to make most of their cubicles unusable for the next few weeks. Management's solution, he told me, was to cram all the office workers with their laptops into the conference room in the meantime.

"My boss is letting me work from home one of those weeks," he said with his head dropped, pointing at the ceiling with a single index finger.

"Why not the full three?" I said, my voice suddenly sharp and loud.

Even as I asked, I already knew the answer. In my cynical eyes, it was the same reason they would make a fuss about non-alcoholic beer. Kester just threw up his hands in defeat and returned to his new drink. Meanwhile my chest was vibrating and my breathing became heavy. All it took to trigger me was the thought of spending an entire day at an office; it filled me with an intractable sense of dread, once which I would happily concede as generational, but it was genuine.

I took a drink to cool off and began to see my friend's plight in more of a comic rather than tragic prism. Then I started to crack up, and I told Kester while fighting back unexpected laughter to just, "do what I did, and don't go in!"

Kester's square, Lego-shaped jaw got tight and his face hardened, and his eyes seemed to ask how I could utter such a question.

"And get fired like you did?" he said harshly.

A more socially adroit individual would have recognized the tongue-in-cheek sheen to my tone, which was evidently lost on him. At least at that moment it was, because immediately after he spoke his eyes widened like a child's would after uttering an obscenity to their parent, instantly realizing the mistake.

I dipped my face into my drink to conceal my smirk. This wasn't something I should be making light of.

Perhaps I was too easygoing and should have cared that he tried to insult me. What really bothered me was he thought I cared given that—as I had told him repeatedly—my day jobs are nothing more than a source to fund my greater calling. Although, in his defense, I had not looked for an audition in months, ever since I won that baseball parlay.

Regardless, I didn't let him get to me, and with my head still tucked and lips pursed on the rim, I picked up my beer and took a little sip, then pulled up fully and started to lean back, relaxing my arms over the edges of the booth's leather.

Kester sat uncomfortably, it seemed, in a rigid pose with his hands folded inward, shielded underneath the table, now fully aware of his overreaction, and of his vulnerability to a reprisal by me.

"Nobody complained," I said, "when about five months in, I didn't show up on

Wednesday, Thursday and Friday in succession, and simply logged on from home. Same thing next week, and still no complaint!" I exclaimed proudly, with a mischievous grin spiraling across my unshaven face. "But I started to get greedy and over the span of about a month, I don't think I went into the office at all. I was still working—just from home. And still bringing in the best numbers out of everyone."

"When did they finally call you out?" Kester asked.

"The following month or so my de facto supervisor messaged me. She sent it a little after nine but I didn't see it until I checked my computer an hour later because after I'd log on, I'd typically go back to bed. She said, 'Hi, Stringer' and I typed back 'Hi.' Then she said something to the effect that I had not been adhering to the three-day minimum work-in-office policy. After that, she sent me a message saying, 'is everything okay?'"

"What did you tell her?"

"The truth. I'm more productive at home, but also that I'd start adhering to the policy."

"But you didn't."

"Nope."

"Why not?" he asked, his face contorting, brows furrowed so forcefully his entire countenance sank and hung like a bulldog's. I thought for a moment.

In my mind, I had rehearsed the professional reason; as an actor, I'm better off without full-time employment.

Never before had I articulated the actual reason I didn't go back. "It was too awkward," I said at last, "having to switch back. Or at least the thought of it." Then I laughed because it was all hilarious and we left the bar shortly after.

Just as we entered the parking lot, Kester turned to me and said, "What are you doing for the rest of the night?" He tried to sound indifferent, but the timing and eagerness of his voice gave it away. I said I was going to bed.

"Word, yeah, it's pretty late," he said quickly. "I got some friends from work who are thinking of checking out this one arcade bar, so I might go there." He seemed to take a lot of stock in having social events to belong to.

We got to his car, a '97 Miata. "You haven't been to mine in a while," he said, a bit wistfully, I might add.

Then, with excitement and a big, toothy grin, he said, "I'll buy the booze and you can finally do your laundry!"

I lied and told him I'd visit soon. And I felt bad, actually, and shallow, even though he had annoyed me.

He was driving up to LA at least three times a week to visit me. He tried to act and be seen like an adult, and to him that meant—as I had just witnessed—having to sometimes beat your chest over chides to your job's honor and your accountability as a worker.

"A man is his career," Jack Lemmon said in a film based on a Mamet play, and in my opinion no truer line has been said. But at the end of the day, I think Kester was more like a kid who just wanted a friend.

He offered to drive me back, but I had already called a ride. I was planning on snubbing him indefinitely; I would've felt too guilty had he driven me.

He revved up the engine and drove off into the night, and minutes later my driver arrived. The ride back to my place was about ten minutes. To get to the freeway, the driver took a stretch of road that passed my former apartment building, one of those old Hollywood buildings that was probably nice a century earlier. Apparently, both William Faulkner and Janis Joplin were once residents. At the time, I lived there with another actor, who was likely in his early forties. His last name was Gaeta. When he first heard my last name (Kincaid) he thought it was Norwegian (it's not.) On my tour of the unit, he was the one who told me Faulkner lived there.

Trying to sound smart, I asked if he lived there while writing *As I Lay Dying*, the only Faulkner book I've read. Gaeta confirmed he was, although later, I looked it up and saw that Faulkner was working as a screenwriter while living in Hollywood, and had already written *As I Lay Dying* back in Mississippi. Since we were both actors and he was older, I figured his film knowledge may have been as wide-ranging as mine.

That notion was shattered early on. I told him that my parents named me after an obscure character from a Robert Altman series on HBO, who happened to share our last name. He said he never heard of the character, the show, or Altman before. I told him that I admired the work of my progenitor's namesake. He asked me why and the best response I could come up with was that his films felt realistic.

As actors, we all had to support ourselves with other work. While I took the unconventional route of supporting myself through full-time employment and sports gambling, Gaeta did the more traditional path and worked as a food delivery driver.

One weekend every month or so, he wouldn't have access to a rental car and would ask to use mine. I let him use it nearly every time he asked, even though he consistently left the dashboard light on overnight.

During the day, I would see beer I had bought the night before was missing; later that same night he'd knock on my door and tell me that he had accidentally drank mine, and not his own beer.

He seemed upset that I bought expensive beer, when in reality I told him I just bought IPAs. I don't think he knew the difference. Every time he'd stumble in to admit his "accidental" theft, he'd make various remarks about how he was suicidal. Many nights I'd wonder what he was doing in his room. Could he really just watch videos on his phone all night? It bothered me he wasn't hustling more, looking for roles, watching interviews of actors. Maybe he was, but it didn't seem like it. I was scared of him because of how common he was. And in my many nights of indolence I'd think about him, how I could never be like him, but that was never enough.

About six months into my stay, we learned that we had to move out by the end of the month. The owner said we could sell the furniture and take the profits. Gaeta wasted no time and most of the furniture disappeared well before our move-out date. Among other items, Gaeta sold the kitchen table. The buyer had arrived, and I told Gaeta I would help him move it. So, I helped him lift it down to the buyer's truck, and at the end when she wished us good luck in finding a new place, Gaeta replied, "I'm going to be living in a tent actually." She laughed it off but when we walked back to our apartment, he told me he wasn't joking.

We probably spent only a second passing by that building, but it stuck with me well into the night, as it always did.

Later that drive I saw an ambulance barrel down Highland, just before turning onto its intersection with Sunset. As it passed, I started speculating possible emergency scenarios that could have necessitated its deployment, and the only thing that came to mind was some poor soul overdosing. Maybe he took a pill or snorted a line laced with fentanyl. Or maybe he took a fistful of Xanax and chased it down with a couple bottles of Mr. Daniels.

Then another scenario sprang to mind: I imagined that this guy, being driven in an ambulance and all, incurred some horrendous physical injury. In that case he probably needed surgery stat, and painkillers in the interim to assuage the pain. But what if the ambulance, if such a thing could ever happen, ran out of painkillers? Traveling from Highland and Sunset to, let's say, Cedars in Beverly Hills, was about three miles. An ambulance with its sirens blaring would certainly cut down on the time, but every block would feel exponentially longer than normal for someone in that kind of pain.

There'd be a lot of drug dealers between those two endpoints, each supplied with a bevy of opiates and whatnot. Maybe the

EMTs knew some of these dealers from personal excursions. It could be as easy as a phone call. The victim would be howling in pain. What if it was a matter of time before the pain took over? Would they risk their jobs like that? Probably not. The people hired to save you would not take every measure to save you; that was my takeaway as my drive nearly concluded.

I had a strange dream that night. It was about my favorite comedian, Greg Giraldo, who had died years ago. He was a drug addict, but also a Columbia and Harvard Law graduate.

I was on an airplane, flying to and from where I had no clue. I was sitting in an aisle seat. All my dreams had this hazy white veneer to them, as if they were only fleeting moments, ready to dissipate, like clouds of smoke floating into the great ether. It felt transient and ephemeral, as dreaming probably felt for everyone.

Sitting in the aisle seat, I saw a jittery Greg Giraldo hop from one seat to the next. He'd pace across the aisle, ruffling his hair, muttering to himself. Though he was talking to himself, I felt that he was trying to communicate to me. Sometimes he would speak to the passengers in the seats next to him. At one point he was in the aisle seat across from me, next to a portly man in the middle.

"I can't believe there was that fire," he told the fat man.

The man nodded, responding with, "It probably was."

I woke up that morning with no clue as to what my dream meant, but with an overwhelming desire to cry and, despite my best efforts, couldn't produce a single tear.

I had been talking to a girl over the past few weeks or so via a dating app. Things had finally picked up steam, but of course, at the least financially opportune moment.

So, I relegated a promised date at some restaurant to a couple bottles of red wine back at mine.

The girl's name was Ruby; she was a musician, but she probably had some other day job as well, as all us so-called 'artists' do. She had short red hair and for some reason, I associated that look with old-fashioned housewives from the fifties despite her several tattoos and piercings.

She let me know pretty early on into the night that she didn't want to have sex, but did so at a later date. Without the pressure to seal the deal, I spoke more openly and with fewer inhibitions, and with the wine we both got into each other's skin quickly. After the first bottle, she started talking about her tarot cards and asked for my sign. I told her "Scorpion" and she laughed then asked for my moon and all that nonsense. At some point she must have sensed my interest in the subject was artificial and waning, so she segued into her life as an amateur medium.

I didn't buy it at all and asked her pointblank if she was full of it. She looked at me as if I said something like the Holocaust didn't happen.

"A lot of people go to psychics here," she said assuredly, clearly unnerved by my skepticism. She was right. There were psychic storefronts all over town; but I pushed

back on the notion all those psychics communicated with the dead, if such a thing
were even possible.

"Some do," she said. "I'm one of
them."

"You're what?" I asked.

"A medium, like I said, which means
I can speak with spirits on the other side."

I humored her, asking her to explain
how it all went down. She told me one night
when she was fifteen, home alone and sullen
after the loss of her grandmother, Mable, she
started to hear a voice. At first it was faint
and muffled, but then it grew sharper and
more articulate.

Apparently, as the voice materialized it
became indistinguishable from that of her
grandmother.

"What was she saying?" I asked, and
Ruby said that her grandmother, just how
she had done in the living, was accosting her
for her various tattoos and revealing clothing.

"I was offended, but so overwhelmed
with emotion that I started bawling. Then I

heard her say 'stop crying.'" Ruby paused for a moment. "Then all I could hear was the sound of myself crying and nothing else."

"Did you ever hear her again?" I asked.

She shook her head. "Since then, I've only been able to connect through to the other side as a medium. Which means talking to a spirit for someone else, someone they knew, when that person's there in the room."

"Can you prove it?" I said, deliberately trying to provoke the challenge, knowing very well a demonstration would be the only way to expel the skepticism from me. She asked if I wanted to speak to someone from the other side tonight. I said yes.

It didn't take long to get things set up for the "ritual"—lights off, screens unplugged, blinds closed. The room was dark and we were sitting across from each other, I on my office chair, she on the futon, with a small nightstand that served as a makeshift coffee table betwixt us. The only light came from a sliver of the window uncovered by the thin curtains.

We touched hands, resting them atop the counter. She told me all I had to do was think of the dead person whom I personally knew, answer her predominantly 'yes or no' questions, and she would lead the way. Like Twenty Questions in seance form, I mused. With our eyes closed and hands together, I started to think of the person. Five seconds later I opened them and looked at Ruby. Her eyes were still closed, but she was straining the muscles around her brow, squinting, as if struggling to hear the other end of a muffled, static-heavy phone call, but without the phone.

Her grasp on my hands started to weaken, until she let go completely and re-turned her hands to her sides.

She twisted her face awkwardly and shot her eyes open for a moment. "Wait, so you hardly knew this guy?" she asked.

"Not personally, no," I said quietly.

She groaned. "But you've met before?"

"Once," I replied. To her credit, she was narrowing in on my person of interest, even with my curveball of a choice. Still, it wasn't enough to suspend my disbelief. "Will it still work, then?" I asked.

"As long as you two have met, it can work. But the stronger the personal connection, the more likely they will respond." She paused. "You think he'll remember you?"

I shrugged. "Maybe."

She stopped speaking and renewed the strain on her face. Ten seconds or so later, she spoke:

"You two... met at an airport... in Chicago," she said, first unevenly, then with assertion at the end. And she was right. That was how he, the dead man I wanted to reach, and I met. Yet there was no conceivable, rational way she could have known this unless she had prior knowledge of me.

Ironically, or perhaps not, the obelisk that was my skepticism of the mystic did not wobble an inch against the winds of credible spirituality. It was one thing for her to guess the person in my mind, but now she had to convince me that she was somehow speaking to him and could recall our very-real encounter.

She peeked an eye open, and I realized I had not answered her.

"Yeah," I said at last.

"You were much younger," she resumed. "Like twelve. He says—wow, this guy talks really fast—he says you came up to him while he was reading a paper or something. He says he worked as a comedian. Was on TV back in the day quite a bit. You told him you were a fan."

"That's right," I said.

"His name was," she trailed off, "Greg Giraldo?"

I had told this story to everyone in my family, a few friends, and all of my past girlfriends. When she said his name, my immediate instinct was deceit and prior knowledge on her part.

She must have gotten in contact with one of these people from my life, then made a perfect estimation as to whom I would want to converse with from the other side when presented with the opportunity.

I wanted to call her out, challenge her in a vociferous and probably rude manner, but

I remembered the look of offense on her face when I questioned the validity of her alleged psychic powers. To my surprise, that restraint I'd conjured allowed me to entertain the genuine possibility that she did in fact have some sort of power, which I would have had hitherto deemed fanciful and nonexistent.

"This guy talks all over the place," Ruby said. "But he actually remembers you." As she sat there, straining to catch what he would say next, his voice emerged in my head, exactly as I had heard it on the radio and on Comedy Central programming; and as I heard him, I recited the words out loud—the words I was hearing him tell me, in a voice. His voice. Most importantly, it was a voice that did not originate from my own imagination. That was unequivocal.

What the hell do you want, kid?

Ruby and I said it in unison, simultaneously reciting what we had both just heard. We spoke not a second apart, in perfect synchronicity.

I fell back into my chair as my bones shuddered at every joint and ligament conjoined to make up yours truly. That experience, my first time connecting with the 'other side', as I liked to call it, was like taking a thousand tabs of acid. The nascent awareness of an entire realm of existence, one which I had an indisputable connection with, flooded my consciousness. It was overwhelming.

I felt like I had won a thousand parlays in the span of a nanosecond, but the reward was something far greater than money, something touching and infusing into me at the most vital of points, for the beneficence of my soul.

My mind and emotions raced in silence as I basked in a newfound sensation of transcendence, when suddenly I noticed Ruby's eyes shoot open. She stared at me, like a falcon on a mouse miles away.

"Am I supposed to hear him too?" I asked.

"No."

Then I heard him speak again.

You two fucking or something?

Ruby's eyes flickered with disgust and I knew she had heard that. I asked to confirm and she nodded weakly, without looking at me. Clearly, she wanted to stop the seance, or whatever the hell this was. Within seconds she stood up, switched on the lights and began to gather her things.

"Doing this makes me really tired," she said hurriedly. "Sorry, I should have told you that."

Moments later she was out the door. Ruby didn't return any of my calls, and frankly I didn't press too hard. It was obvious she was jealous. But that wasn't important, because I learned not only that she wasn't full of it, but I was full of it. And it was real.

What I had envisioned to be some ill-conceived form of mediation proved to be something far different.

I couldn't fall asleep that night. In the morning the awe had begun to fade, but not the excitement. I wanted to do it again.

I waited until it was dark; my intuition told me this kind of thing only worked at night. I prepared my room exactly as I had the night prior. Then I sat in my office chair and started to think of Greg Giraldo.

My eyes stayed closed for what felt like hours but what was actually just a couple of minutes, and all I could hear was the spinning blade of the ceiling fan and a faint high-pitched bark from one of the landlord's many Shi-Tzus.

When I opened my eyes, I could feel the muscles in my face harden in fury, like after losing big on a clear favorite, as I looked across at an empty futon, as if my interlocutor *should* have been there.

It crossed my mind that a different seating location could make a difference. I moved to the futon, closed my eyes and waited. Once again, I heard nothing other than the faint ambiance of my material surroundings.

From a young age I discovered that the greatest joys in life were fleeting, in a constant state of vulnerability to the pernicious

Murphy's Law. So, handling the transition from the ecstasy of the prior night to what I felt at that moment was, while still difficult, manageable.

"C'mon, Greg!" I yelled jocularly, shooting my eyes open and smacking the leather with my hand. I got up and walked to my computer, searching for a compilation of Greg Giraldo's bits on Comedy Central.

At some point during the video, toward the middle, I recalled Ruby's story about her first time speaking with the dead. She said that after the first time, she could only tap into this special power as a medium.

Admittedly, I thought I was excluded from that sort of limitation, but such was not the case. I had to find someone. Yet the field was pretty thin when it came to people in town whom I knew well. I had maybe two friends, no real girlfriend, and no colleagues. Of those two friends, I hadn't seen one of them in over a year; as for the latter, Kester, I was still feeling ticked off by him. I had to find a stranger.

The question of *who* mattered less than their whereabouts. My first instinct was to pursue the virtual avenues like Craigslist, Reddit, and dating apps, but I was a bit too anxious to enter that somewhat protracted process. I decided the best way was the good old-fashioned way, hitting the dives.

A bar just a block or two away from mine, The Silverlake Lounge, would be my recruiting ground.

It looked a lot smaller on the outside than it did inside. I arrived a bit before eleven on a Thursday, which was a perfect time because there were already dozens of patrons.

They were all in groups; the thought of approaching them made me apprehensive and second guess my decision to refrain from alcohol, so to get a "better connection" with the other side. Only after the fact did I remember that I was already drunk when I did the reading with Ruby.

I stayed to myself, sitting at the corner of the bar, eyeing potentials, and ordering Diet Cokes. Often people would order right next to me, and I'd glance at them as they waited, wondering whether they would like to communicate with a ghost.

I didn't want any dudes, so that cut my options down in half. The only time I interacted with someone else was when a girl was passing me to get to the exit. I stopped her and said this quickly: "Hey, I'm trying to find out whether I'm a medium. Would you be interested in helping me out?"

She just smiled and politely said "No, thank you" as if all I asked her was if she wanted a drink, and continued toward the exit.

A quarter till closing, the bar was practically empty. I was finishing the remains of a Diet Coke when the bartender came to me.

"You come here just for soda, man?" he said playfully. He was big, a tan skinned bald man with a jet-black goatee full of tiny hairs that pointed in all sorts of directions. He was wearing a black tank top, and his bulging arms were covered with ink of religious imagery. I had the sense he looked much older than his actual age.

I looked up and made a half smile.

"That's not why I'm here," I said.

I thought for a moment, wondering if I should play along and make some stupid joke, lie and say I'm an alcoholic, or tell the truth. I chose the last option. "Can I tell you something that's going to sound crazy?" I asked.

He nodded while fidgeting in place for a bit, as if initiating some sort of defense mechanism. I explained in detail what happened the prior night, and why I wanted to find someone at the bar. At the end of my story, I looked up to see his reaction. From his expression, I sensed he thought I was pulling a practical joke on him.

"So, I need someone else in order to do this," I said.

The bartender narrowed his eyes. "You don't have a friend or something?" he asked.

"I'm from out of town."

"You're crazy, man," he said, with a quick laugh.

"That's why I didn't order any booze. I love beer!" I said.

"What, you can't get drunk or something when you do it?"

"That's my guess."

He thought things over for a moment. Then he leaned in and looked me straight in the eyes, inches away from my face.

"You can try it on me," he hissed through his teeth. "But if I find out if you're just messing around, I'm gonna be pissed."

"I don't know if it'll work or not," I stammered back. "But I promise you, I'm not making this up."

He continued to stare at me. Then, slowly, he pulled back, and his eyes finally seemed to trust me. The fact that he took this so seriously told me he wanted to connect with someone who meant a lot to him, someone he knew personally, and that made me nervous. I knew he wouldn't hurt me, but I was worried about the emotional pain he would feel if things did not work out.

He asked where this was supposed to go down, understanding that I wanted to do it tonight. I told him my place, and that it was just a couple blocks away. He told me that the bar would be closing in ten minutes, and he'd be ready to leave in about twenty, but I was welcome to wait. I told him I was fine outside.

The last wave of patrons began to shuffle out. I got up from my seat, told him my name and extended my hand; he returned with his and told me his name was Pablo. Like he said, he was out the door ten minutes later.

It was a short walk to my place. I didn't have the urge to make small-talk, and neither did he. Again, I told him my place was close, and that was it. When we stopped at the front of the gate, he looked surprised, not realizing I only occupied one quadrant of the house. Thankfully none of the dogs were out, and nobody was on the streets or pulling up in a car, to see what I think must have been a comical sight of us two walking up those stairs.

I opened the door and let Pablo enter first. "You gotta take care of your place, man," he said, looking around at the cramped mess. He took a seat on the futon, while I grabbed a water bottle from the fridge, and drank damn-near all of it in a swig. I offered my guest one, but he refused.

I started to make the preparations, explaining my rationale to Pablo as I switched the lights and turned off the screens.

He didn't seem to care too much about the logistics. I took my seat at the office chair and swiveled it to face him with the nightstand between us. Pablo looked away, his eyes heavy and wary. He was lightly rocking back and forth, clenching his knees in his palms. I could see him in his mind, playing through the course of events. It reminded me of the fear I felt just before talking with someone after a bitter feud.

"We don't have to do this if you don't want to," I said. Of course I didn't mean it; I just wanted to sound appropriately thoughtful. Really, I was calling him a coward, and I kind of hoped he picked up on that. He studied me for a moment. "It was not an easy relationship," he said. "It was messy." It sounded like he was trying to warn me, but that didn't make sense. I saw him as scared and apprehensive. He was venting to me, treating me like his shrink. I didn't like that.

"Like I said, we don't have to do this if you don't want to."

He narrowed his face as he stared at me squarely, seemingly showing his contempt for my tone. Then after a moment, he pulled back and broke the stare. "Never mind," he said finally.

He stopped rocking; his body steadied itself in place, and I took that as the cue to go forward.

"What I need you to do is to start thinking about the person," I said. "You don't have to tell me who this is. Just think about them."

He nodded. "I need to see your hand," I continued, extending mine to the table. He brought his over. "I'll let go eventually," I said.

It could've felt weirder if I had let it, but I was focused. I knew if I concentrated, I could make the connection again.

I closed my eyes and everything became darker than it already was. The slivers of light made their faint imprint against the backdrop of blackness that my closed eyelids produced. I didn't pay attention to the dancing gradients that befell my lack of vision, and I didn't think; I was just there, but I was aware that I was there. The rugged—and for some reason, damp—texture to Pablo's hands became like a hat I forgot I was wearing.

I heard his breathing, a heavy wheeze. It had an almost musical quality to its rhythm; each breath rumbled like the base note of a trombone.

In the background was a faint whining noise, like a high-pitched woodwind, and it started to get more prominent as the breathing subsided into the background. And the high-pitched music started to sound less and less like it was from a musical instrument and more like a human voice. It still had a reverberation like an echo, but with each beat, the sound became a tad more decipherable.

I couldn't make out the precise words, but the voice came from a middle-aged woman.

"There's an older woman," I said. "She's loud and keeps repeating the same thing."

I moved my hands away from Pablo, not even glancing to see his reaction, as I strained to hear more closely. I began to hear it as a two-word phrase; the first word was the subject, and the second qualified it.

Then the first word became clear to me; it was his name.

The woman was saying his name, over and over again. And she kept following it with the repeated second word, and I realized the second word was not in English, but Spanish.

"She keeps saying your name and then another word, over and over again."

"What's the second word?" he asked quickly, and I told him it was something in Spanish. I began to sound it out. "*Mee-ho, mee-ho.*" Then Pablo leaned back in the futon and started to look away toward the window.

I asked him what it meant, the second word, and he said it was a term of endearment his mother used to call him when he was a little kid.

I heard her voice again, and this time her words were more enunciated, as if she figured out I wasn't a native speaker. After she finished, I tried to translate as best as I could.

"She also says: *Ramon tay man-da sahlou-dos.*"

My studies of Romance languages from high school told me this probably meant, "Ramon says hi," and when I recited it out loud, I saw silver droplets amidst the darkness trickle down Pablo's husky brown face. His face sunk into his hands and began to weep.

I watched Pablo cry, which he did without shame, and did not feel embarrassment for him.

Although I did not know what had specifically upset him, other than the reading of his mother. I figured that would be sufficient enough to provoke such a response. But the name "Ramon" was what triggered the tears.

It was like asking a question you knew you didn't want to hear the answer to. That's how it felt when I asked Pablo, after he stopped crying, about Ramon. He didn't look up, nor respond.

I repeated myself, and he remained silent.

"Who was he?" I asked for the third time, now with a cracked voice and watery eyes. There was no reason for me to share his tears, yet there I was. Pablo relented—maybe because of my response and persistence—and he told me about Ramon, leaving about a half hour later.

Pablo and I inadvertently formed an emotional bond. The wisecracks of my comic hero simply did not move me the way hearing this man's loved ones spoke to him, and their tragic story.

I found what I was seeking to discover, or re-discover, and this time, I felt its toll, understanding more accurately the post-reading fatigue Ruby had mentioned. It was like skipping straight to the hangover.

I'm sure Pablo returned to that same bar in Silverlake the next day. I'm sure If I ever went back there and saw him, all would be fine.

But I don't think I want to see him again. For my own sake.

I put aside the spiritual world, fearful of witnessing a revelation like I had that night, one that left me limited to my bed, a catatonic, without an appetite for days, and hysterically teary. It was too much to risk repeating.

Coupled with that, matters concerning the material world—food, rent, sports bets— flooded my thoughts to the point of drowning any vestige in me that harbored interest in further exploring my psychic capabilities. And so I returned to the world of sports gambling, of moving the needle one inch forward, then back, multiplied however many times over.

Still, it was enough to pay rent for the next few months. In that time, I also found some minor acting work.

Life moved on.

Autumn, my favorite season, finally arrived. With the cool weather around me, I started to go on more walks through my part of town.

From my home, I would start down the sloped road and walk past a couple houses until I reached the stretch of Sunset that cut through Silverlake. I would take that stretch until I reached East Hollywood, just about, and then turned around and start the same path in reverse back to mine.

On the way back from one of these walks, just as I started up the block to my home, I saw a thin girl with a beautiful mess of red hair. She was standing by the gate, and her head was tucked over her phone. She saw me walking toward the gate, put away her phone, and then walked slowly toward me, looking shyly. "Hi, excuse me," she said. "Are you Stringer?"

"Yeah," I said, my voice shaky. It was hard not to get nonplussed when an attractive stranger, from literally off the street, approached you and knew your name.

She looked a bit thrown off by my response, as if expecting me to say more. She cleared her throat and waved a friendly hand in the air.

"My name is Daphne," she said.

"Hi. Have we met?" I asked.

"No, not quite." She thought for a moment, then smiled at me. "I've kind of been stalking you."

I thought she was too pretty to be a stalker.

That's what I could have told her, and she might have laughed.

But a line like that felt too heavy-handed for my taste. I figured she was making some type of silly joke, but still I was taken aback.

I let out a forced laugh, as I suppressed my face from contorting in confusion, and said uneasily, "What are you talking about?"

She shook her head, quickly and reassuringly. "Okay, stalking isn't the best word."

She paused. "I've seen you around this part of town a lot, and I've been hoping to meet."

"That's nice," I said. "Why?"

"I sort of eavesdropped on you one night," she said. She proceeded to tell me she was a regular at the bar where Pablo worked.

Apparently, she overheard our entire exchange that night, the one which led me to doing my second psychic reading.

My eyes widened and I couldn't help but chuckle lightly, and she did too. It was hard for me to play dumb and keep a straight face in situations like that, which couldn't help but feel comical, and it seemed to be the case for her as well.

"I haven't seen you there since. That's why I came here," she added.

"So, what, did you follow us back here that night?" I said teasingly. Now that I knew why she wished to see me, I became more relaxed, willing to make riskier jokes.

She gave me a modest look and her small wavering eyes instantly told me she had, and then with an embarrassed giggle, she confirmed it.

"That's what I figured," I said to her with congenial-sounding fake laughter. I think I played it cool, but in my mind, I was shocked she had actually gone so far as to follow us back. But it didn't truly upset me, because I was attracted to her, and I think she was to me.

"So, um, how far did you get in? How much did you hear?" I asked awkwardly, unsure whether she only followed us to the gate, or went past as well.

"Don't worry," she said. "I only went to the gate."

"So, you didn't hear me give the reading?"

"No."

"So then how do you know I'm a psychic?" I asked. "Just from overhearing me at the bar and seeing us go back, and you believe it?"

She thought for a moment. "I guess so, yeah. And Pablo, he looks and acts like a different person. Way more zen, if that makes sense." She paused again. "I mean, it did happen, right?"

I shrugged my shoulders and smirked, and said quietly, "I mean, yeah, it did," and we both laughed.

"Well," she said, looking at me softly with curious eyes, "I was hoping you could maybe give me... a reading."

I looked at her and took in the sincerity of her eyes and voice, almost folding to it. I sensed this question would arise as soon as she brought up what she had overheard. And I knew that my answer would disappoint her.

"I'm sorry," I said, "but it's not really something I like to do anymore."

She raised an eyebrow and stared at me, as though deeming my response insufficient.

"Why not?" she asked.

I moved my lips, readying to give her a succinct response, but I stopped before any words were uttered. Giving a quick, perfunctory response, I realized, would have made me feel arrogant.

That wouldn't fly, as I wanted to continue talking with her. "You wanna get a coffee somewhere?" I asked, and she said yes. We walked around the corner to the closest coffee shop.

"So, stalker," I said to her as we sat at a table with our drinks. She both smiled and frowned, in the way that told me she liked my joke but recognized it poked fun at her. I leaned over my espresso and spoke quietly, "I've only done two of these psychic readings before. The first one—I mean honestly, I wasn't even trying. I just heard this one comedian I loved, talking like he normally did. It was amazing, but it wasn't, like, emotional."

"And the second one you did with Pablo; I'm guessing that one was?" she said.

I nodded, shifting away from her gaze. As soon as she said that my face started to feel heavy, and my skin went cold. "Yeah. I don't know how well you know that bartender," I said. "Seems like you know him at least as an acquaintance. And you've probably known him longer than I have. But that night, I got to know him *very* well. Just in the span of an hour. You learn a lot about people, really *too much* about them. And it's heavy. Very depressing. That's what I learned. You know, I could probably make a fortune off this, but it's just too heavy." I stopped, hoping she wouldn't ask me to get specific.

Did she really need to learn, as I unwittingly did, that Pablo killed his own brother during a bar fight, and that their mother died of grief?

I didn't think so.

She looked away from me, her lips puckering. "I get it," she said coolly.

I sensed her disappointment. Yet I heard she had not truly considered my reservations.

Although how could she, truly? I wanted to give her the benefit of the doubt because ultimately, due to my attraction to her, I didn't want to let her down.

At the same time, I considered myself a sensitive soul. I didn't need the weight of another devastating family secret on my shoulders.

"Who did you have in mind?" I said, my curiosity and arousal taking hold, and she said she wanted to communicate with her father.

I dropped my face and sighed, because that sounded precisely like the type of reading I didn't want to do.

"It's not what you think," she said. "I hardly knew him. He died when I was like three. My mom remarried and I consider him my dad."

I took a sip of my espresso then smiled at her, as congenially as I could in that moment. "Okay, but here's the problem," I said. "Anything involving parents, no matter the context, gets emotional."

She tapped her fingers on the table like a keyboard player as her eyes anxiously fluttered, searching for a response.

"But it's not," she said. "I hardly even

remember him. I just remember him making me laugh as a kid. I'm sorry, I'm just... I'm just really curious, and I can't help it." She stopped speaking and waited for my response.

I ran my hand through my hair, still apprehensive, and saw her eyes follow my fingers intently, eager for my response.

"He didn't die some tragic death, right?" I asked in a matter-of-fact way. She quickly threw her hands over her mouth to conceal her laughter, and seeing her laugh made me laugh as well. I didn't tell her yet, but by then, I had decided I was willing to help her.

"No, no, no" she said, shaking her head, still laughing. Once she settled down, she looked at me and said, "but isn't all death tragic in a way?"

"I don't know," I mumbled back. Was she being aphoristic or profound? I couldn't tell. Even if it were the former, it would not have dissuaded me from acquiescing to her request.

We found ourselves in my tiny abode later that night, with the lights out, seated across from one another. I grabbed her hands and closed my eyes, starting to hear what sounded like a match getting lit. I peeked my eyes open to see if it were coming from the material world, from Daphne, but she was motionless.

Then I started to hear coughing, and grumbling, coming from a gravelly voice. This turned into words and sentences, talking, in an accent that had hints of a Midwestern rhythm to it.

"This guy's smoking. Said your mother always badgered him to stop, but even on the other side, he can't." I told her this, and she gently squeezed my hand in response.

He was talking about his and Daphne's mother's whirlwind romance, which entailed eloping in Las Vegas and an extended honeymoon in Iceland.

This guy was clearly a wild card, and successfully seduced his prim and conservative lover, much to the dismay of her parents. I had no clue what he looked like, but I envisioned someone built along the lines of

George Clooney, but with messier hair and a perpetual leather jacket.

"He asks why you stopped playing cards," I said, and I couldn't help but smirk. "What, did you guys used to play Go-Fish or something?" She chuckled nervously. I don't think Daphne knew how to react. Everything I told her she had already heard but did not remember.

I think she wanted it to be more emotional than her history allowed. He said he was happy for her and her mother, and I told Daphne that, and in response she closed her eyes and spread her face with relief. She moved her lips in silence; I think she said a little prayer.

As I continued listening to him speak about Daphne and their family, Clooney, my name for the ghost, suddenly changed topics.

This is what I heard him say:

Alright, enough with this sentimental shit. Okay? Listen to me, kid. Here's what you're going to do: take the over on the Lak-

*ers game tonight. Take the over on the Lak-
ers game. Oh, and in case I wasn't clear,
take the over on the Lakers game. Thank you
very much.*

He even had the same wry sense of humor that I associated with Clooney. But, he
stopped speaking, and I knew he was gone.

As I was processing that jarring non se-
quitur, I must have been frowning expres-
sively and muttering confusedly to myself.

I should have tried to conceal my countenance, because Daphne, looking startled,
asked if I were okay. I told her I was fine
and was only trying to concentrate as the
'connection' was fizzling out, which technically was true.

I looked at her and told her it was over.
Daphne looked back at me with awe, be-
holding what she had believed up until then
was an act of the impossible. Her eyes
looked at me invitingly and her body
became relaxed, and I sat next to her. She
stared at me, and I back at her, then slowly
we both leaned forward until we collided
softly into each other's lips.

Taking off her clothes was quick and easy, as her loose baggy garments had hung freely and provocatively from her thin waist and over her pebble-sized shoulders. Each of my arms stretched out on opposite sides of her neck, and as my hands grazed her shoulders, I looked down at her, admiring the way her hair draped and swirled around her head, like patterns on an Iranian rug, and how the very tips of the strands gently tickled the tops of her breasts. My blood sank.

In that moment I felt immortal; no psychic powers nor any million-dollar parlays could matter as much as this did. I descended, spreading her legs apart with my torso as I entered. "Oh," she moaned. "Oh, Stringer."

Waking up that morning I instantly recalled the hazy image of her gently shaking me from my slumber, to say she was going home, but would text me soon.

The thought of her and our night made me smile and feel content, and I closed my eyes once again, lying there blithely. Not long into my reverie did I remember the voice of Daphne's late, truculent sounding father—Clooney the ghost—and his impromptu gambling pick, which was to take the over on the Lakers game.

I didn't make the bet last night; right after Daphne and I had sex we put on some old interview from my phone and both crashed shortly after.

I probably wouldn't have made the bet if I had the opportunity. He struck me as more of a rambunctious player looking to get a vicarious thrill out of gambling than as a seer. But I still checked the NBA scores from last night's games. The Lakers beat the Raptors, 110-106, for a total of 216 points scored. I typed in "Lakers Raptors picks" on the search bar of my phone and clicked the first link that was listed. From it, I saw the over/under had been listed at 212, and incidentally that publication had told their readers to take the under.

This meant Clooney predicted a winning bet. Maybe, wherever he was, he had access to the scores in advance. Could he predict another winning bet? I wondered.

Also, this was a man who seemed to care more about gambling than communicating with his daughter.

In my head I tried to chicken and egg this scenario: was he a degenerate to begin with, or, did the years since his death cause him to lose feelings for his daughter?

It never occurred to me that the dead could lose interest in the living over time, just as the living did for the dead.

Daphne and I had hit it off, so I didn't think it would be hard to arrange a follow up to our first date.

I had to come up with a believable reason as to why I wanted to keep speaking with Clooney. Would she want me to keep giving her readings of him? Though astonished by the first go-around, I anticipated subsequent readings would be less enthralling for her.

Above all, I hoped they wouldn't provoke any strong emotions. From either of us.

A week later I took her to a bar within walking distance from mine. She was still excited with my reading, and I played on that energy, although personally I no longer had that zeal. I think it was fair to say that it was quickly replaced by greed.

I told her I couldn't stop thinking about it, and that I had to do it again that night. She made no objection, and we returned to mine after finishing our last round. We wasted no time in assuming the psychic position. I held her hands and began to hear his familiar voice.

"Is he there?" I heard Daphne say, and I nodded. "What's he saying?" she asked impatiently. This is what he said:

So you two are a thing, huh? Well, you better be good to her. She's my only daughter. That means she means a lot to me... Right?

"He asked about our relationship," I told Daphne.

Yeah, yeah. Good, tell her that, he said sarcastically. *I know that's what you care about. You care about her, not some game, a baseball game, MLB, Blue Jays.* He paused. *Take the line on the Blue Jays and buy a place to take her back to that's nicer than this dump.*

His voice began to dissipate from my mind, and soon all I could hear was my own breathing. I told her that I lost the connection, and got up to turn on the lights and use the bathroom. From my phone, I placed the bet he had given me seconds earlier. When I placed it, the game was set to start five minutes later, as if he had anticipated the timeliness.

I took his advice on betting large and put down five hundred—all I had left in my account. Daphne gave me a sweet look as I returned, instantly dispelling my fear that she was upset given the small duration of the reading. I knew she wouldn't want to watch a random baseball game, so I let her decide on the show, knowing it would give me more latitude to use my phone throughout the night to check the score. She put on a reality television show from years back about girls who lived in the Playboy mansion.

Normally I would have objected, as I considered Hugh Hefner to be a cretin, but extenuating circumstances advised otherwise. The show was a bit under an hour long. When it finished, I lied and told her I liked it, and wanted to keep watching. She perked up and put on another. And over the course of that episode, and the subsequent ones we watched, I perennially checked the score, each time seeing the Blue Jays widen their lead until defeat became impossible.

It hadn't occurred to me to check the odds until after the fact. When I did, I saw the odds were completely against the Blue Jays. I remembered the stats from the prior game Clooney suggested; that pick wasn't highly favored either.

That was all the convincing I needed. As I reveled in my winnings, with Daphne asleep on my futon, I decided to go onward, full-throttle.

Over the following six weeks I communicated with Clooney through Daphne.

I never figured out how he did it, but each time he gave me winning bets. Cumulatively, this led to a sizable increase to my net worth. It was nothing short of a miracle.

But it was a challenging miracle to maintain, as I had to uphold a perpetual insistence to communicate with him, which Daphne needed to humor. I saw no other way to do this without entering a relationship with her and making her my girlfriend.

So that's what I did, and it felt like the right thing to do, although I knew any true relationship between us was destined for failure. I was attracted to Daphne, and I enjoyed spending time with her, but I don't think there can be love on either end in a situation like that.

I took Daphne on dates more frequently, longer ones that didn't just involve food and eating. We learned more about each other. I told her about my rearing in Upstate New York, and my activist parents who were borderline hippies, the types who would admonish my watching of someone like Piers Morgan as flirtation with the right wing. She learned about my background in acting, and I'm sure that my less than effusive talk on the subject confirmed my lack of passion. She learned about all the jobs I did to make money, and how I hated working in an office, yet hated service jobs even more, which is what most struggling actors did.

Of course, I didn't need those jobs anymore, as nearly each time we hung out, I communicated with Clooney. I framed it in terms of my selfish desire to communicate with him further, and she bought it, and was happy to oblige, initially. I tried to frame it as appealing to her desire to continue communicating with him, which she seemed to appreciate, at first.

Daphne was a couple years younger than me, born and raised in the Bay Area, and went to college at UCLA. She majored in Communications, but had been working at a cupcake store since graduation. Her mother was Chinese with family from Taiwan, which was why I found it strange when I visited her place and saw she had a bust of Mao Zedong in her bedroom. Not to get political or anything, but that would be like the Confederate decorating its outposts with portraits of Lincoln.

Her dad, the ghost I called Clooney, was something of a big shot. He capitalized on the tech boom in the late '90s, got rich off of it, but sadly succumbed to his deadly vices.

He left Daphne and her mother, an activist-type graduate of Berkeley, (we had that in common, similar parents) a lot of money; that was good, because I gleaned from Daphne that her mother's employment situation was flimsy.

The man she re-married, Daphne's step-dad, sounded like a nice guy, but frankly he seemed like a bit of a loser. That was just my opinion.

I was glad to see that Daphne seemed to like him and accept him as her father because her birth father, as much as I hate to admit it, didn't seem to care about her too much.

In each of the first several readings, he would talk about her. I would relay what he said to Daphne. Then, he would give me the pick. After a while he stopped mentioning Daphne completely, and just gave me gambling picks. So, I began to make up what he was allegedly communicating to me, and told these lies to Daphne.

Thankfully, I had learned a lot about him, both from Daphne and from hearing him speak, so it wasn't too hard to pastiche his voice.

Still, I liked to keep his purported comments broad and vague, just to be safe. Eventually, I developed other types of excuses. Sometimes, I'd tell Daphne that I couldn't hear him. Or, during a reading, I would sort of sigh and say, "Yeah, I guess he doesn't really feel like talking right now." Concurrently, in my mind, I was trying to remember every pick he gave me. Over time that became more difficult, as eventually he began to give multiple picks, and they could get specific.

I was back to the parlays!

The parlays consisted of imperceptible picks. When he first gave me a bet that I considered preposterous, I think it was having the Diamondbacks sweep the Yankees, I asked him to reaffirm his suggestion with the pretense of making it look as if I were asking to re-confirm something he was saying about Daphne. During that reading, right after he gave me that crazy pick, I said out loud, "Oh, really? Are you sure?" I made sure my voice sounded excessively inquisitive, so to fool Daphne. I told Daphne I was taken aback by his comment. "What did he say?" Daphne asked, and I replied, "He said I couldn't say," and she looked confused. In reality, Clooney never directly responded to my questions. It was a one-way line, I learned.

I'd get restless the nights we didn't communicate to the other side, and Daphne would notice. Sometimes, I'd try to make the connection without her knowledge. We would be lying on my futon, spooning, and while I'd hold her, I would try to establish a connection—close my eyes, concentrate. But it never worked; it always ended with Daphne wondering why I was suddenly murmuring to myself and holding her tightly. Really, it was all for me. Not just the readings and gambling, but our entire relationship. That was just the truth, and part of me did feel bad. I excused it by spending lots of my newly acquired money on Daphne: nice dinners, clothes, even a weekend getaway to Joshua Tree. Yet the part of me that felt bad only grew. I'd compensate with expensive dates but my reward was psychic traveling rather than sex, and that bothered her. I think that traduced our relationship until it was purely transactional, with no remnants of romance left.

I spent a week home over Thanksgiving break. Daphne did the same, and we returned that Monday following the long weekend. Hypothetically, I think those in a healthy relationship should feel restless after an extended time apart from their partner, and yearn to see them as soon as possible. I only felt that way because I wanted to make more money, and the only way I could was through Daphne. And I made so much money from her. I lost interest in just about everything else. It was like a drug. And like a good addict, I only cared about getting more of that drug—more readings, more money, more wins—despite the diminishing returns.

By that point, Daphne was genuinely weirded out by my insistence to psychically connect with her father. I could have only guessed that she was starting to develop suspicions about my motives.

I picked her up the next day, Tuesday afternoon, in my Lexus sedan, which she had helped me choose. It was finally getting colder, and there were forecasts for rain. I was driving, and she was sitting shotgun. We hardly said anything to each other. At one point, I caught a glimpse of her admiring the upholstery. She was running her hands across the tan leather, petting it like a fluffy cat.

"This car is so nice," she said, then paused for a moment. "Why don't you move out of that place already?"

"It's on my to-do list," I said.

She didn't respond and returned to stroking the leather.

We found a diner in Hollywood and parked there for lunch. I ordered a turkey club, while Daphne had some sort of salad. "So back home was alright?" I asked her, right after we placed our orders. She nodded and began to recite what I already knew, what we had discussed via text and phone that week while apart.

I hated discussing topics already covered over text, but that was all we had left to talk about. I already knew she had a middling time. She could never really have a good time anywhere because she was in a bad relationship.

Once our food arrived, we went quiet, an excuse to keep to ourselves. As we neared finishing our meals, I looked at her and asked, "Did you tell your family about it?" She stopped chewing and looked at me.

"Why would I do something like that?" she said.

I started cracking up, smiling cheekily. Apparently, she had no room for humor. "It was a joke," I said, rolling my eyes.

She looked at her bowl of greens and poked at it with her fork, puckering her lips innocently. "I mean, we decided not to do that anymore, anyway."

I froze. Everything in the room went quiet. "We did?" I asked, for I certainly did not remember agreeing to that.

She sighed. "Yeah, we did, actually."

I replayed the nights, and nothing came up.

"When?"

"Over break, you moron," she said, and there was no playfulness to be found in her tone.

Just contempt. "We were on the phone. I guess you don't pay attention to our calls at all."

"Thanks, I figured that. I meant which day."

"Day before Thanksgiving."

Hearing those words took me back to late Wednesday night on the sofa of my family's den, an old movie, and a shiny bottle of a scotch I had bought for them. They noticed its value. And they saw my new clothes. I think I wore the same beige jacket and black jeans every prior visit, for at least the past year. Now I was wearing corduroys and a sweater from Oscar de la Renta. I was also decidedly chipper. It was nice seeing my parents and not having to worry about money at the same time.

None of these expensive material objects could be explained by alleged acting success on my part. There'd be a role to show for it. And I didn't have a job. I knew if I did not give them an excuse soon into my stay, they would start to think I'm selling my body, or dealing drugs, which they would excuse for the underprivileged, but not for me.

It wasn't the fact that I got incredibly loaded off that scotch later in the night that stood out. It was that I had not thought of a reason beforehand to tell my parents why I now had so much money. But then the answer presented itself in a beautiful form of synchronicity.

"I have been dating a girl," I told them, seated in the den, each of us a few drinks into the scotch. "And, well, she's rather rich."

Relief swept both of their faces. Their shared, almost identical responses told me I was in the clear. It was a partial truth. Yet, lying made me feel guilty, and led me to drink more than I should have. I didn't consciously go, "I feel bad about lying so I am going to drink more than I should." It just happened.

It was strange… Typically my recollection becomes foggy after a night of heavy drinking, but I can still make out the general course of events, and the mood of the room. In the morning, I will replay them in my mind, while I'm lying in bed and wishing that a magical glass of ice water would appear by my side to assuage the pain of the hangover. I do remember the hangover, but that was it. The pain was so excruciating that I never did replay the prior night's events. Nor did I discuss it with Daphne, until now. I was drinking, and drinking, and then things went blank.

But while I strained to remember as we sat in the diner, I tucked my head down, and my eyes caught a glimpse of the plates the diner served. They were a standard white ceramic, but had faint gray streaks across the middle, almost like a lightning bolt. These plates were identical to the miniature ones my mom had served various hor d'ouvers on that night, off of which I consumed copious amounts of food, which I am now recalling that I threw up in our bathroom.

And my call with Daphne finally came back to me. It occurred in the bathroom. Right after I vomited, I stayed in the bathroom because I was afraid there was more to come. I sat and leaned against the edge of the bathtub.

I was looking at my phone screen, scrolling through early Black Friday deals, when the screen started to gyrate on an axis, and I went spinning with it. I dipped my head over the rim of the toilet and let it out. That time, I knew it was over, but then Daphne called and I answered it, still lying on the bathroom floor. I began to recall the mood.

Daphne had gone into a fit of hysterics, claiming that I only cared about her dad, and

not her, which of course was true. And she
felt bad that I seemingly wanted to communicate with him more than she did. I'll
admit remembering that made me feel bad,
as I sat across from her in that Hollywood
diner even though I told her that night, as I
am now remembering, that I would give up
psychic readings with her father.

"You're right," I told her, reaching for
my cold coffee. "I'm remembering everything now." She didn't say a thing.

We looked at each other in silence.
Daphne's face was glowing under the light
at our table. I wondered, in an alternate scenario, if everything were the same except for
my attraction to Daphne. I'm not sure if I
would have developed feelings for her; I
think at that moment, at the diner, I would
have just got up and left. She was telling me
that all that was left for us… was us. And I
had to decide if that was enough.

And I think it was. At least, that's what I
decided then, and felt now. But it was like
quitting drugs, or alcohol. Name the vice.
You tell yourself it's going to be the last

time, even though you may not truly believe it, or at least haven't processed it. When I first agreed to end the readings, over that drunken phone call, I had neither believed myself nor processed what I had said. Yet, I was ready to call it quits. I had made enough money. I did see the slightest possibility for the chance of a real relationship, with the psychic business behind us.

Still, I wanted to go out on my own terms. I told Daphne that I would stick to my (drunken) word, on the condition that she would allow one last psychic reading of her father. She agreed.

Later that weekend I took her to a Michelin Star restaurant. It was an apology in the form of a grand gesture. In any event, I knew it would make going through with the last reading that much easier. It was a nondescript building on some road in Culver City. It was the most expensive dinner I had ever bought up to that point, though I knew that I would recoup the cost that same night.

After our dinner we went back to mine.

As agreed, we prepared to do a reading with Clooney. We assumed the position, and moments later I started to hear him mumbling to himself. This is the part where he would tell me the gambling picks, and I would tell Daphne what he was saying, which became made up. At first, when I would lie, Clooney would chuckle and make some sly remark. But eventually he stopped.

That night, all I heard from him, other than the unintelligible mumbling, was the gambling picks, a parlay. This was the parlay he gave me:

Lakers game over; Bruins game under; spread on Yankees; spread on the Mets; and the line on the Rockies. The last part of the play was the last thing I ever heard him say.

After he left, I opened my eyes and looked at Daphne. At first, she seemed nonplussed, as if expecting to have become overwhelmed with emotion.

"He says he knows that this will be the last time we do something like this," I told her. "He said he's happy for us and will always be watching."

I think I sold it a bit too well, because Daphne's eyes started to water and her face turned red. That made me uneasy. Not that I was unaccustomed to her crying; in this case, the crying was the result of a false pretense. I took a seat on the futon next to her, threw my arm around her shoulders, and played us some videos on the TV. With my other hand, I checked the start times for the respective games on my phone.

From gambling with Clooney, I had earned approximately fifty grand. Initially, I kept the bets at the amount of my first one, which was five hundred dollars. Gradually I increased the amount by small intervals, and then plateaued my typical bet at one grand. I did this for all subsequent ones, until my last.

The following day Daphne left in the morning, and I placed the parlay at five grand. But right before I confirmed, I decided to change the bet to the maximum amount allowed, and the maximum amount I could put in, which was coincidentally fifty grand. I hadn't put a single penny toward paying off my debts and student loans, other than my old car loan, after which I bought the Lexus.

I checked my phone later that afternoon to see the scores, and nearly had an out-of-body experience when I saw them. I stopped watching the games because their outcomes had always occurred as Clooney had predicted. That's why I was beyond shocked when I saw my wager lost.

Fifty grand gone.

I spent the remainder of that day and the entirety of the following weekend again in a near catatonic state. Amidst my wallowing, I tried to make sense of things. First, I immediately ruled out mishearing Clooney. I had become exceptional in my capacity to memorize his picks. Since he gave me the picks, and I placed them correctly, that meant for the first time he had given me an incorrect pick. And I wondered why, and how. Had his clairvoyance run its course? Had he deliberately misled me? Part of me gave weight to the notion that Clooney was getting a bit jealous with all the money I made, thanks to him. But why would he help me in the first place? Was he fed up with how I was taking advantage of Daphne? Jealous of my earnings? My mind searched for answers, as I remained woefully fixed to my bed, only getting up for food and outhouse usage.

As the weekend came to an end, I started to feel the vitality that I had lost creep back into my skin. Once my fit of despair had ended completely, I knew I had to communicate with Clooney again, which meant I had to see Daphne. It had been a day and a half since I had last seen her. I grabbed my phone to text her and saw she had already messaged me.

Actually, she texted me several messages, probably close to fifty. And called just as many times, too. But I had my phone on silent, as I was too depressed to engage with anyone, let alone my girlfriend. I called her back and apologized. As I scrambled and stammered for an excuse, I noticed Daphne

sounded particularly relaxed, even mono-
tone. She brushed off my absence like I was
only away from my phone for a couple
minutes. She asked if I wanted to meet at
this dive bar she discovered near me; she
was already there, and I left mine minutes
later.

On the drive over I thought about her
curious tone. It wasn't beyond the realm of
possibility that she was breaking up with
me. If she were, that would've been the tone
I'd expect her to carry. And maybe it would
be for the best. Except it wouldn't, because I
still needed to communicate with Clooney,
just one more time. I just needed to hear
from him once more. Whether I got no response, a legit bet, or a bad one, I would
learn just a bit more about his motives and
be that much less in the dark. Maybe, if our
relationship ended, she would keep letting
me do the readings. But I doubt she would
put up with that.

As soon as I entered the bar, I saw
Daphne sitting at a booth, faced away from

me. Across from her sat another red-head I knew.

Ruby.

When we met eyes, Ruby gave me a scowl and nudged Daphne, who turned around and stared at me intently and angrily as I walked over. They both gave me the same look, as if they bested me in some dispute over power and were going to tell me all about it.

"What's going on?" I asked.

"You're disgusting, Stringer," Daphne said bitterly. She wasn't even looking at me. "That's a little harsh," I replied plainly. I wasn't in the mood for coddling after losing that bet.

She turned to Ruby, who was smirking at me. "Ruby told me everything."

"Okay," I said, and I could see that the indifference in my tone bothered them.

"Aren't you curious how we know each other, Stringer?" Ruby asked.

"Yes, please tell me!" I said suddenly with irritation.

Daphne stood up and pushed me with her thin, tooth-pick sized arms. "He was just giving you gambling tips!" she shouted. She did not look as strong as she felt.

I blinked at her, confused, then toward Ruby. All she did was evince this sort of self-congratulatory smile.

"Daphne hired me, Stringer," Ruby began, "because she thought you were hiding something from her, during your readings with her dad."

"Why didn't you talk to me about it?" I asked Daphne.

"I couldn't prove anything. That's why I went to her," she said. "But I knew something was up."

"In my defense," I started, "I didn't ask him to give me any bets. He just did. And they were always right! How else do you think I paid for all those dinners?"

Ruby chortled. "All *we* had was some cheap wine back at your place." She sounded envious.

Daphne gave a tepid laugh in acknowledgment.

I came clean. "At a certain point, he stopped bringing you up," I said.

Daphne frowned, hurt by my truthful admission, I suppose. And when I saw her response, it made me understand Clooney's logic a bit more. I had already determined that his ultimate goal was to punish me. All it took to do that was one wrong gamble on my part, one where I would lose everything, no matter how many wins I had scored on the lead-up. All the money I had accumulated in the process, only to be squandered. Clooney was kind of a dick, I realized. "I don't know what you guys want me to tell you," I said, with a casual, deliberately flippant shrug. They stared at me, without saying anything. There was nothing left for me to do or say, so I turned around and left.

On the drive back I kept thinking about one more bet. One more reading from Clooney. Maybe he'd have given me a pick that would've hit. Maybe I could have figured out a way to outsmart him, pick the inverses of his choices, or something.

As I neared home, I began to think about going back to gambling the old-fashioned way. And I couldn't fathom the idea for long. If I couldn't go back to the old ways, then I wouldn't gamble at all.

If only I had saved a little more, bet a fraction on that last parlay, something. I didn't know if it were good or bad that I did not use any of that money I won on a new dwelling. Probably the former, as I could continue with my cheap payments, unlike the ones I had for my car, which I would probably have to sell at some point.

Money was the thing I had to think about now. Acting was not going to bring me any dough, although I knew I had to start resuming that hustle. I thought of all the day jobs I used to do that I hated, and then the full-time office jobs, which I hated a bit less, even though inevitably I could never bear going into an office repeatedly. I had my problems set out for me.

An obvious solution would be to make money, a fortune in fact, off my psychic powers. But I decided that not only would I not profit off of it, I would abscond with my psychic dealings all together.

It was clear this had to be done as soon as I left that dive bar. My decision, I think, was mostly so not to risk upsetting my emotional state like that ever again. I learned this with Pablo, but also with Daphne.

You might think she had more to do with greed. Greed certainly played its part. But I had, I truly believed, destroyed love. On top of that, I don't think that guy cared for his daughter at all. Not that it was wrong of him. It just didn't occur to me that would happen. And that too was heavy. But in the morning, that decision seemed selfish to me, and unfair. At least, insofar that I knew that I had to postpone giving up the ghost, just so I could use my powers one last time.

It had been months since I last saw Kester. My frail ego had hampered me from setting up another rendezvous, on account of my shortcomings, and his immaturity. In my defense, I had become quite busy. He kept inviting me over but, at some point, stopped. Our dialogue eventually became reduced to sending each other the occasional link to a funny picture or headline. But I knew he would have liked to hear about my experiences those past few months. That's why I decided to do one last reading. I accepted that giving him a reading would be upsetting to me; it was not a rule, but they almost always ended up that way. It would ultimately be nice for him, and that was that.

I drove down to Orange County to visit him. Over that afternoon I explained to him earnestly my newfound ability, and what had happened as a result. He believed me, of course, and I told him I wanted to do a reading for him. And he agreed to it.

I'm not quite sure what exactly happened, but unfortunately my power seemed to have worn off by then. And so, there was no reading. Regardless, I think my friend was glad to see me.

Photo courtesy of Jamie Benjamin

Aleks Stajkovic Jr. is a writer based in Los Angeles who is originally from Madison, Wisconsin. He writes fiction and screenplays, often blending elements of comedy, horror, and the supernatural in his work. Psychic Gambles is his debut book.

9 798993 691718